*For Serena*
Derek

*For Katia, Gaelle & Joël*
John

First published 1984 by
Walker Books Ltd,
17-19 Hanway House,
Hanway Place, London W1P 9DL

Text © 1984 Derek Hall
Illustrations © 1984 John Butler

First printed 1984
Printed and bound by L.E.G.O., Vicenza, Italy

British Library Cataloguing in Publication Data
Hall, Derek
Panda climbs.—(Growing up)
I. Title   II. Butler, John   III. Series
823'.914[J]   PZ7

ISBN 0-7445-0131-8

# Panda Climbs

### By Derek Hall

### Illustrations by John Butler

**WALKER BOOKS**
LONDON

Panda loves to play with his mother. Sometimes she gives him a piggy-back and then he feels as tall as a grown-up panda.

Soon it is dinnertime.
The grown-ups eat lots of
bamboo shoots, crunching the
juicy stems. Panda likes
to chew the soft leaves.

The grown-ups eat for such
a long time, they always
fall asleep afterwards.
Panda scampers off to play.
He rolls over and over in
the snow and tumbles
down a hill.

When Panda stops at
the bottom he cannot see
his mother any more.
But he sees a leopard!
Panda is very frightened.

He scrambles over to the
nearest tree and climbs up.
Panda has never climbed before,
and it is so easy! He digs his
claws into the bark and goes
up and up.

Soon, he is near the top.
Panda feels so good up here.
And he can see such a long
way over the mountains and
trees and snow of China.

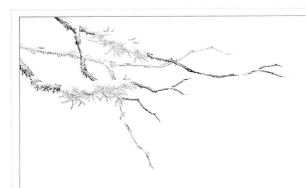

Panda hears his mother
crying. She is looking for him.
He starts to climb down.
But going down is harder
than climbing up, and he slips.
Plop! He lands in the snow.

Panda's mother is so happy.
She gathers him up in her big
furry arms and cuddles him.
It is lovely to be warm and
safe with her again.